POEMS BY
Tony Mitton

ILLUSTRATED BY
Mary GrandPré

SCHOLASTIC INC.

New York Toronto London Auckland Sydney
Mexico City New Delhi Hong Kong Buenos Aires

ISBN 0-439-56210-4

Text copyright © 1998 by Tony Mitton. Illustrations copyright © 2003 by Mary GrandPré.

All rights reserved. Published by Scholastic Inc. SCHOLASTIC, SCHOLASTIC PRESS, the LANTERN LOGO and associated logos are trademarks and/or registered trademarks of Scholastic Inc.

12 11 10 9 8 7 6 5 4 3 2   3 4 5 6 7 8/0

Printed in the U.S.A 08   First Scholastic paperback printing, September 2003

Arthur A. Levine Books hardcover edition published by Arthur A. Levine Books, an imprint of Scholastic Press, March 2003. The text was set in 13.5-point Benguiat Medium. The artwork was created with pastels on toned printmaking paper. Book design by Mary GrandPré and David Saylor

Contents

For Elizabeth, Doris, Guthrie, Tiggy, Dad, and Ruth with love —T. M.

For Chopper and Charlie and the Curly Spud —M. G.

PLUM

Don't be so glum,
plum.

Don't feel beaten.
You were made
to be eaten.

But don't you know
that deep within,
beneath your juicy flesh
and flimsy skin,

you bear a mystery,
you hold a key,

you have the making of
a whole new tree.

MY HAT!

Here's my hat.
It holds my head,
the thoughts I've had
and the things I've read.

It keeps out the wind.
It keeps off the rain.
It hugs my hair
and warms my brain.

There's me below it,
The sky above it.
It's my lid.
And I love it.

flightpath

BUZZ...

The reason why the fly annoys me, as it does, is that, however hard I try, I can't ignore its

Puzzled Pea

I'm just a pea
in a plain pea pod.

But there's something about
little me that's odd.

For, although like the others,
I'm a plain, green pea,

they are all *them* . . .

while I'm
just *me*.

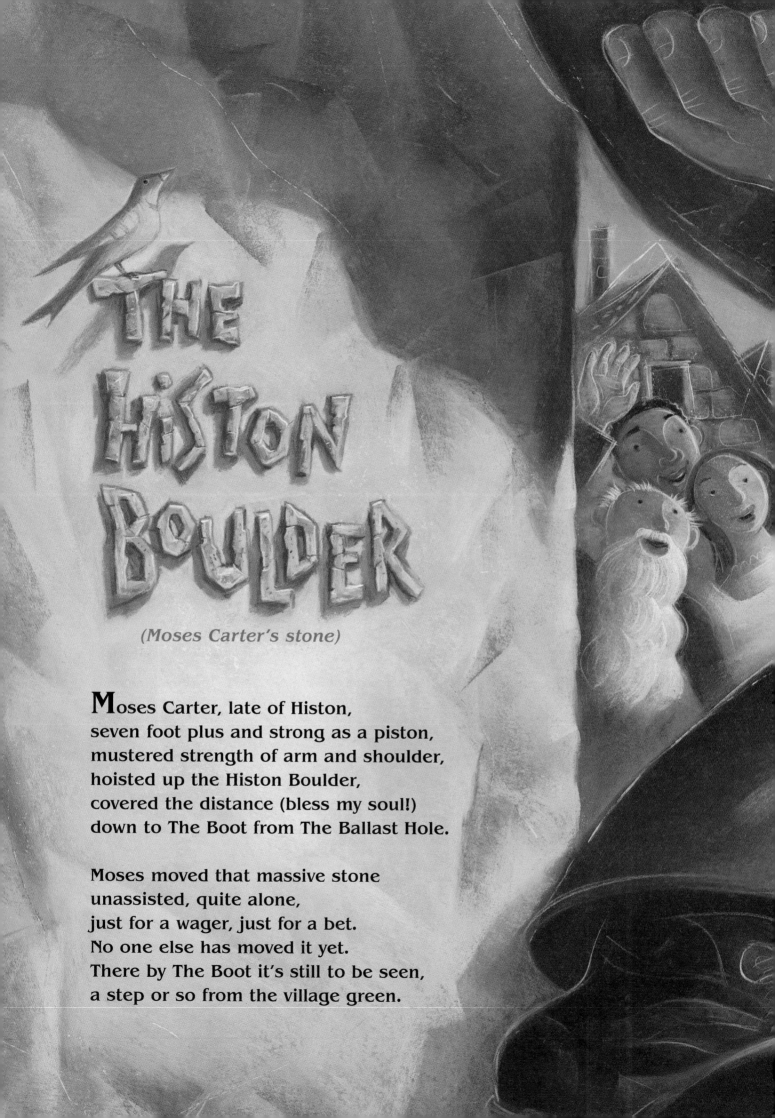

THE HISTON BOULDER

(Moses Carter's stone)

Moses Carter, late of Histon,
seven foot plus and strong as a piston,
mustered strength of arm and shoulder,
hoisted up the Histon Boulder,
covered the distance (bless my soul!)
down to The Boot from The Ballast Hole.

Moses moved that massive stone
unassisted, quite alone,
just for a wager, just for a bet.
No one else has moved it yet.
There by The Boot it's still to be seen,
a step or so from the village green.

Moses Carter, great of height,
fond of children, kind, polite,
munched his dumplings, chewed his beef,
passed away to general grief.
If giants were all so calm, so tame,
they wouldn't earn so bad a name.

Moses Carter, dead and gone,
has left behind his heavy stone.
Nothing else, apart from that,
but a single boot and a stovepipe hat.
In Histon Churchyard now he lies
in a grave they dug him, giant size.

Shore Music

When the wind is calm
and the moon is full
and the waters softly swing,

you may see the mermaids
sit by the shore
as they comb their hair and sing.

Your ears may long
for their strange sea song,
but do not tread too near.

At the slightest sound
of a foot on the ground
they will dip . . . dip . . .
disappear.

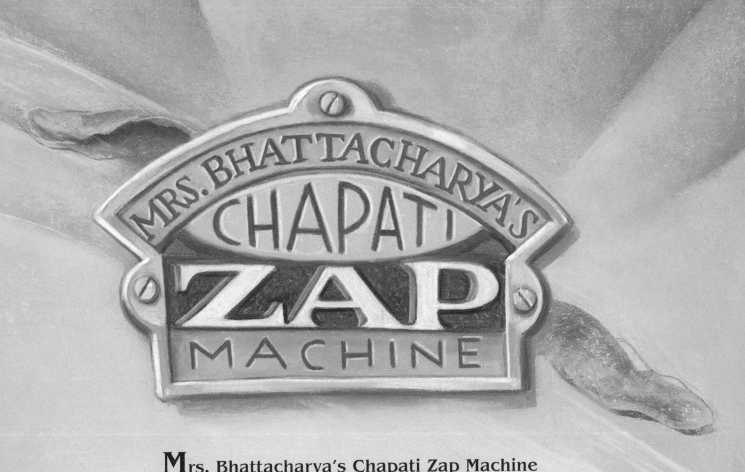

Mrs. Bhattacharya's Chapati Zap Machine
is marvelous, amazing. It's the best
   there's ever been.
It sizzles hot chapatis
   at a most amazing rate,
then flicks them spinning through the air
   to land upon your plate.

Mrs. Bhattacharya's Chapati Zap Machine
has buttons, knobs, and levers
   in blue and red and green.
It mixes fine chapati flavors:
   peppered, spiced, or plain,
then shoots them out in showers
   like a hot chapati rain.

Now Mrs. Bhattacharya's
   machine is very new,
so even Mrs. B can't say
   for sure what it will do.
And yes, it rather looks as if
   she's getting in a hurry
as twenty hot chapatis
   make a landing in the curry.

But Mrs. Bhattacharya's
   a brilliant engineer.
She tinkers with a spanner
   and she listens with an ear.
She twiddles with a lever
   and she fiddles with a dial.
"I think that puts the trouble right,"
   she whispers with a smile.

Mrs. Bhattacharya's Chapati Zap Machine
is going to the Palace by Appointment
   to the Queen.
The queen wants hot chapatis
   for a royal dinner guest,
and someone told her Mrs. B's
   chapatis are the best.

Mrs. Queen and all her guests
   are sitting down to dine.
The president of Zarnia has come,
   and all looks fine.
A bell is rung, the doors swing wide,
   and suddenly is seen . . .
Yes! Mrs. Bhattacharya's
   Chapati Zap Machine!

Mrs. Bhattacharya is pressing Button Blue.
The ground begins to tremble . . .
   the Zap Machine goes Phooooo!
Now Mrs. Bhattacharya is pressing Button Red
as six big hot chapatis
   flip out swiftly past her head.

One flies up and perches
   on the crystal chandelier.
Another settles neatly
   on an admiral's right ear.
And one with lots of butter,
   a lovely golden brown,
flies straight toward the queen
   and punctures, PLOP!
   upon her crown.

One attacks a general
   and slaps him on the head—
he snorts into his sherry
   and his face goes cherry red.
Another meets a duchess
   and causes her distress
by landing on her shoulder
   and sliding down her dress.

But one especial big one,
   the largest of the lot,
all seasoned, spiced, and buttered,
   all round and steaming hot,
performs the worst thing possible,
   a terrible disgrace:
It squelches on the president
   of Zarnia's solemn face!

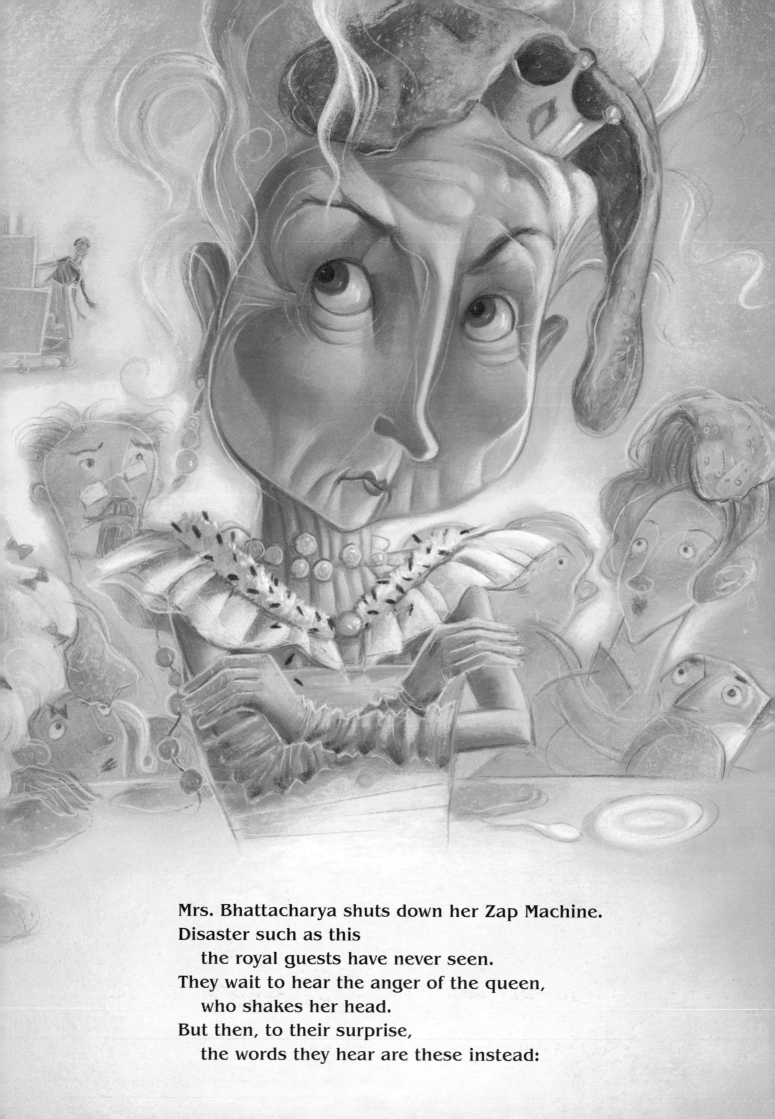

Mrs. Bhattacharya shuts down her Zap Machine.
Disaster such as this
   the royal guests have never seen.
They wait to hear the anger of the queen,
   who shakes her head.
But then, to their surprise,
   the words they hear are these instead:

"Hurrah!" shouts Zarnia's president.
     "And double hip hooray
for Mrs. Bhattacharya's
     Chapati Cabaret!
Is this a British Bunfight?
     I've heard of these before.
Keep going, Bhattacharya!
     I'd love to play some more!"

Mrs. Bhattacharya
     looks straight toward the queen,
who nods, "Yes . . . start it up again,
     your . . . 'cabaret' machine."
Next moment Zarnia leaps up high
     to catch a fast chapat,
then throws it in the air and shrieks,
     "A splendid catch — HOWZAT!"

Then bit by bit the guests forget
    they're grown up and polite.
They start to dodge and duck and catch,
    like children, with delight.
And bishops, bigwigs, baronets,
    and butlers . . . everyone
begins to feel, since they were small,
    they haven't had such fun.

And now to cut a story short,
    a party with the queen
is really quite a different thing
    from what it used to mean.
The guests all turn up gleefully
    with faces bright and keen . . .
for Mrs. Bhattacharya's
    Chapati Zap Machine.

So Mrs. Bhattacharya
    is famous in the end,
and if you plan a party soon
    please don't forget to send
for Mrs. Bhattacharya, who,
    as I've just heard tell,
is setting her machine
    to pop out poppadoms as well.

It's fabulous, it's marvelous,
    it's big and bright and clean.
Its buttons, knobs, and levers
    are blue and red and green.
It's chosen by Appointment
    to Her Majesty the Queen.
It's Mrs. Bhattacharya's
    Chapati Zap Machine.

1

If you blow
I will grow
to a trembling ball.
I'm a bubble of breath
in a shimmering shawl.

If you lift
I will drift
like a wisp of the air.
Then I'll burst with a gasp
and I'm simply not there.

②

I am only
a bubble,
the ghost of a ball.

If I'm caught
then I'm naught,
I am nothing at all.

I am only
a bubble,
a shimmering sphere.

If I land on your hand
I shall soon disappear.

Hullo, pussies, come and see.

I'm the heftiest ever feline flea.

I'm somewhat fat and six foot three.

So I pity the cat that catches me.

Elegant Elephant

Come to the Elephant Delicatessen.
Sample the delicate elephant treats.
Savor the flavor of elephant edibles.
Taste what the elegant elephant eats.

Come to the Elephant Delicatessen.
Tickle your trunk with a truffle or two.
Toy with a tidbit of tree-leaf in aspic,
O Epicurean Elephant, you!

Delicatessen

Come to the Elephant Delicatessen.
Elephant aliments spill from our shop.
Pick up a packet of Pachyderm Poppadoms.
Sip at a schooner of Elephant Pop.

Here in the Elephant Delicatessen
Are exquisite rarities gathered from far.
So come for a great gastronomical lesson.
We're just by the Elephant Superbazaar.

(P.S. We are serving free
E L E F F E R V E S C E N C E
delivered today from our
Elephant Spa.)

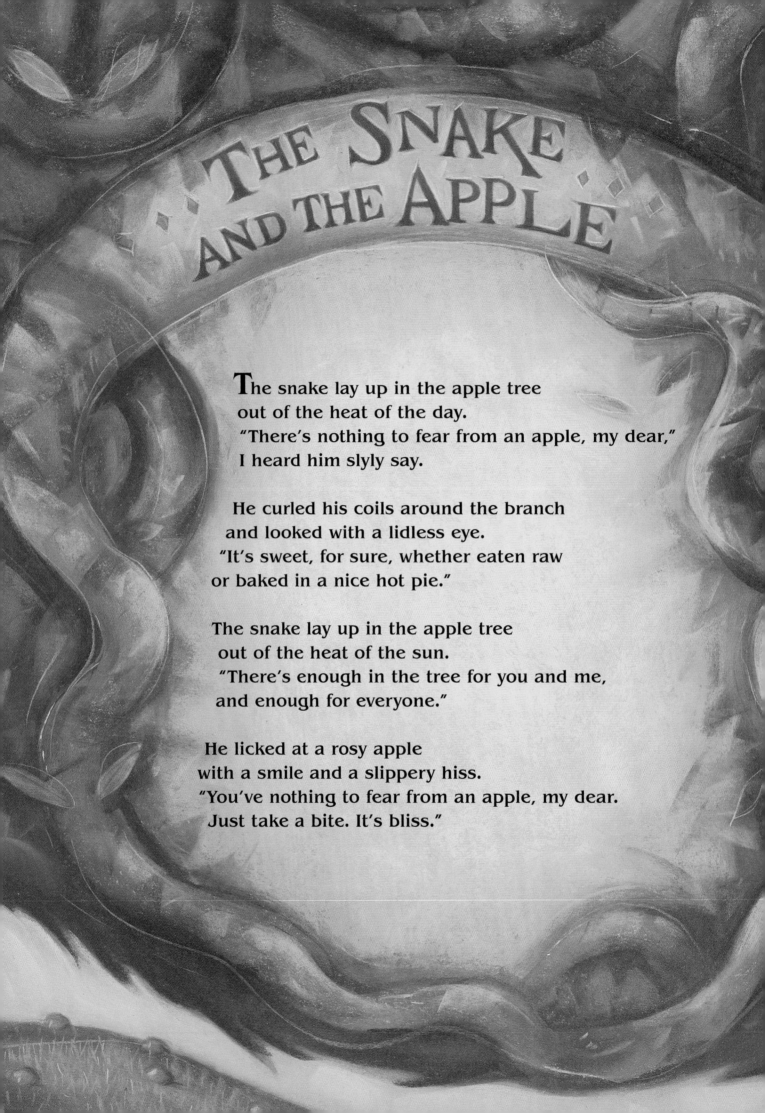

THE SNAKE AND THE APPLE

The snake lay up in the apple tree
out of the heat of the day.
"There's nothing to fear from an apple, my dear,"
I heard him slyly say.

He curled his coils around the branch
and looked with a lidless eye.
"It's sweet, for sure, whether eaten raw
or baked in a nice hot pie."

The snake lay up in the apple tree
out of the heat of the sun.
"There's enough in the tree for you and me,
and enough for everyone."

He licked at a rosy apple
with a smile and a slippery hiss.
"You've nothing to fear from an apple, my dear.
Just take a bite. It's bliss."

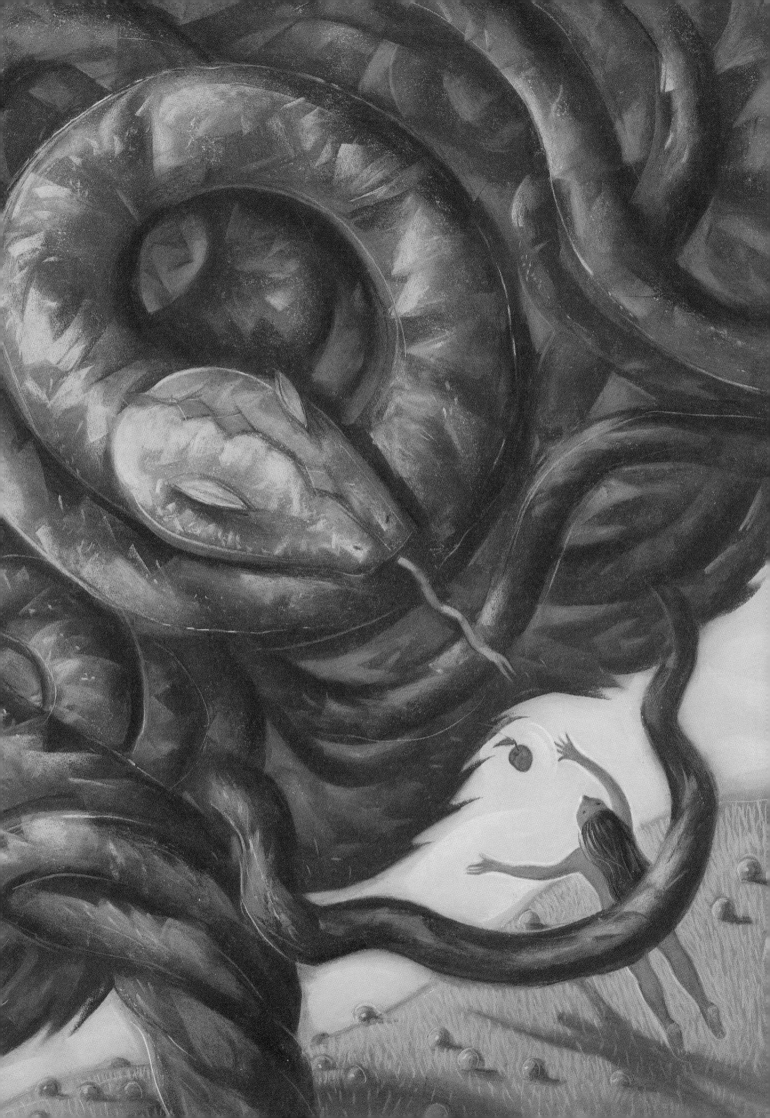

THE MINSTREL

(overheard on a cottage doorstep)

I'll strike you a strain
from a silver string.

*I'll do you a dance
that's fit for a king.*

I'll breathe you an air
on a flute of gold.

*I'll tell you a tale
that's wise and old.*

I'll fiddle you a jig
that's wild and funny.

*I'll find you an almond
dipped in honey.*

AND THE MAID

I'll tickle you a rhythm
on a magic drum.

*I'll show you a taste
of a sugarplum.*

I'll pipe you a tune
on a whistle of wood.

*I'll bake you a cake
that's warm and good.*

I'll sing my song
in a strong, clear voice.

*I'll give you anything.
Take your choice.*

GROWING

Today
you may be small.
But one day
you'll be tall,
like me,
maybe taller.
You won't
fit into your bed.
Your hat
won't fit on your head.
Your feet
will fill up the floor.
You'll have to bend down
to come through the door.
You'll be able to reach
to the highest shelf
(and I can't do that now,
myself).

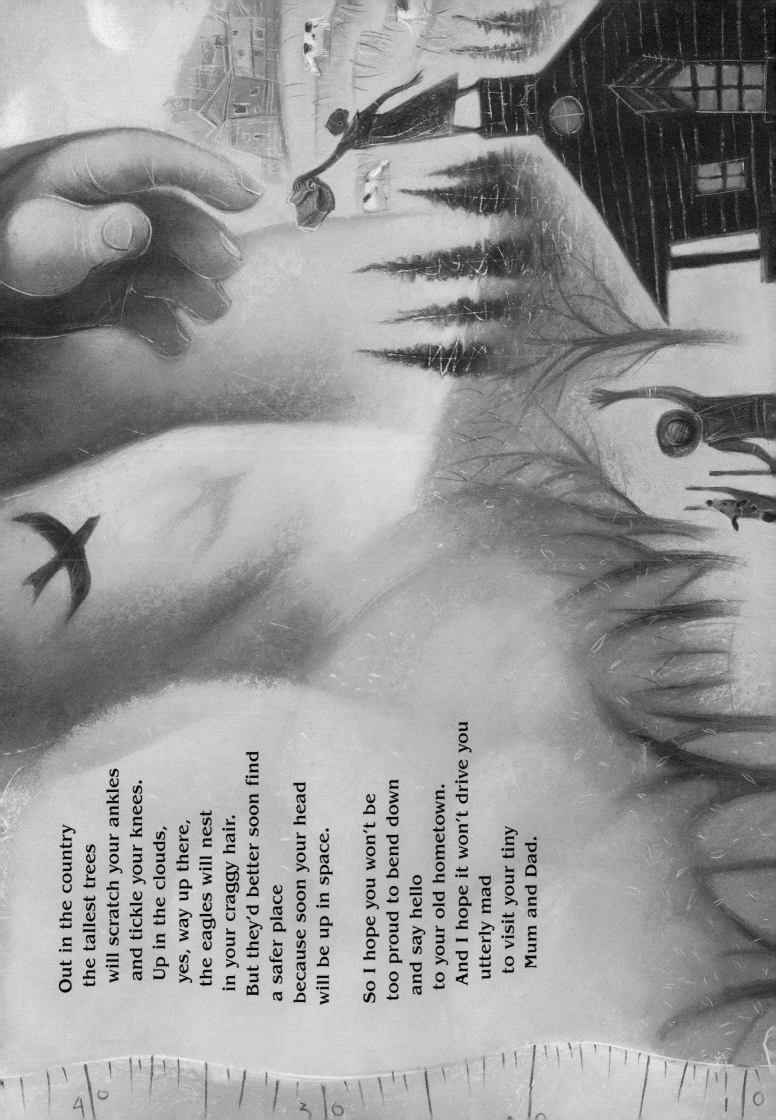

Out in the country
the tallest trees
will scratch your ankles
and tickle your knees.
Up in the clouds,
yes, way up there,
the eagles will nest
in your craggy hair.
But they'd better soon find
a safer place
because soon your head
will be up in space.

So I hope you won't be
too proud to bend down
and say hello
to your old hometown.
And I hope it won't drive you
utterly mad
to visit your tiny
Mum and Dad.

Green Man Lane

As I went walking down Green Man Lane
I met a stranger there.
His clothes were all of foliage
and tangled was his hair.

He did not pause for pleasantry
nor bid me how-d'ye-do.
He only stood with eyes of wood
that pierced me sharply through.

The leaves crept close around me.
The earth pressed at my feet.
I felt the breeze upon my skin,
my heart's insistent beat.

Never a word the stranger spoke,
though his stare was keen and clear.
But the leaves around us rustled,
and my blood ran thick with fear.

And the leaves around us shivered
as a sudden silence fell.
And I felt the life of the ragged wood
in that dark and greeny cell.

I felt the thirst of each living leaf
as it lapped at the air for breath.
And I felt the search of each striving root
as it sifted life from death.

A scent of blood and fear sprang up,
a grip of beak and jaw.
And slow things moved in rich decay
beneath the forest floor.

Then a small bird sang out sharply
as the sunlight filtered through.
So I stepped out into the meadow
beneath a sky of blue.

And I saw how the field of bearded wheat
had grown from green to gold.
Then I thought of the man in the leafy coat,
with his look so keen and bold.

But whether the sun be shining bright
or the hedge be wet with rain,
I'll hesitate before I pass
along that lane again.

St. Brigid

As Brigid was walking
the old narrow track
she passed by a baker
with bread in his sack.

She put out a hand
from the fold of her cloak,
and these are the words
she softly spoke:

*"Please give me a loaf
for my sisters and me,
and we'll share it tonight
as we sit to our tea."*

and the Baker

But the baker, he muttered
and shook a mean head.
*"If you want to eat, sister,
then bake your own bread."*

She looked in his eyes then,
but all that she found
was a stare that was hard
as the stones on the ground.

So Brigid passed quietly
along the hard track
as the bread turned to stone
on the baker's back.

Song of the Wizard's Imp

Catch me if you can,
I'm a whisper of air,
a splinter of sunlight
    that's gone if you stare.

    Catch me if you can,
    I'm a shadowy patch,
    a rustle of cobweb
    that's gone if you snatch.

    Catch me if you can,
    but be sure that you dare,
    for I nestle to rest
    in a wizard's warm hair.

    Yes, catch me if you can,
    but be warned I am weird,
    for I settle to sleep
        in the wizard's white beard.

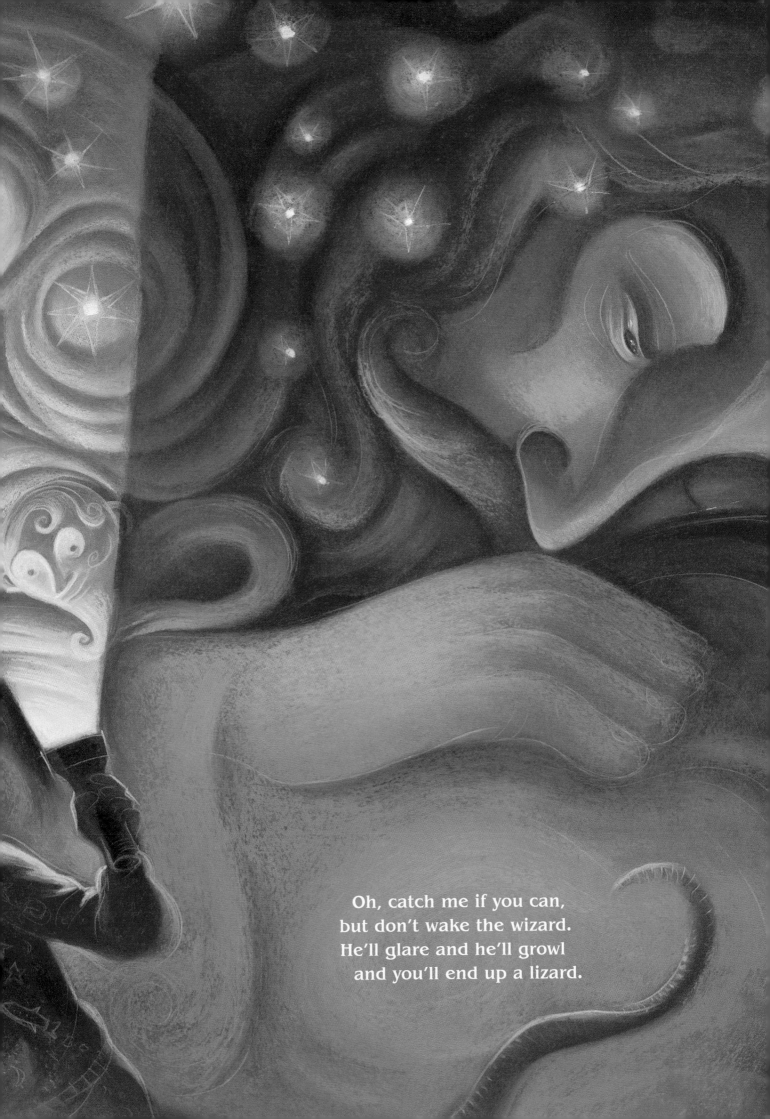

Oh, catch me if you can,
but don't wake the wizard.
He'll glare and he'll growl
and you'll end up a lizard.

What is under the grass, Mummy,
what is under the grass?
    Roots and stones and rich soil
    where the loamy worms pass.

What is over the sky, Mummy,
what is over the sky?
    Stars and planets and boundless space,
    but never a reason why.

What is under the sea, Mummy,
what is under the sea?
    Weird and wet and wondrous things,
    too deep for you and me.

What is under my skin, Mummy,
what is under my skin?
    Flesh and blood and a frame of bones
    and your own dear self within.

What is
Under?

Mrs. Rummage's Muddle-Up Shop

When I tried to ask for a lollipop
in Mrs. Rummage's Muddle-Up Shop,
she stopped and said, "I think I might . . .
Let's see . . . I saw one here last night.

"Now, just where did that lollipop go . . . ?
Where exactly . . . ? I don't know.

"Oh dear. This really just won't do. . . .
Is there something else I can get for you?"

And when I said,
        "I think it's there . . ."
            she just looked blank
                and scratched her hair.

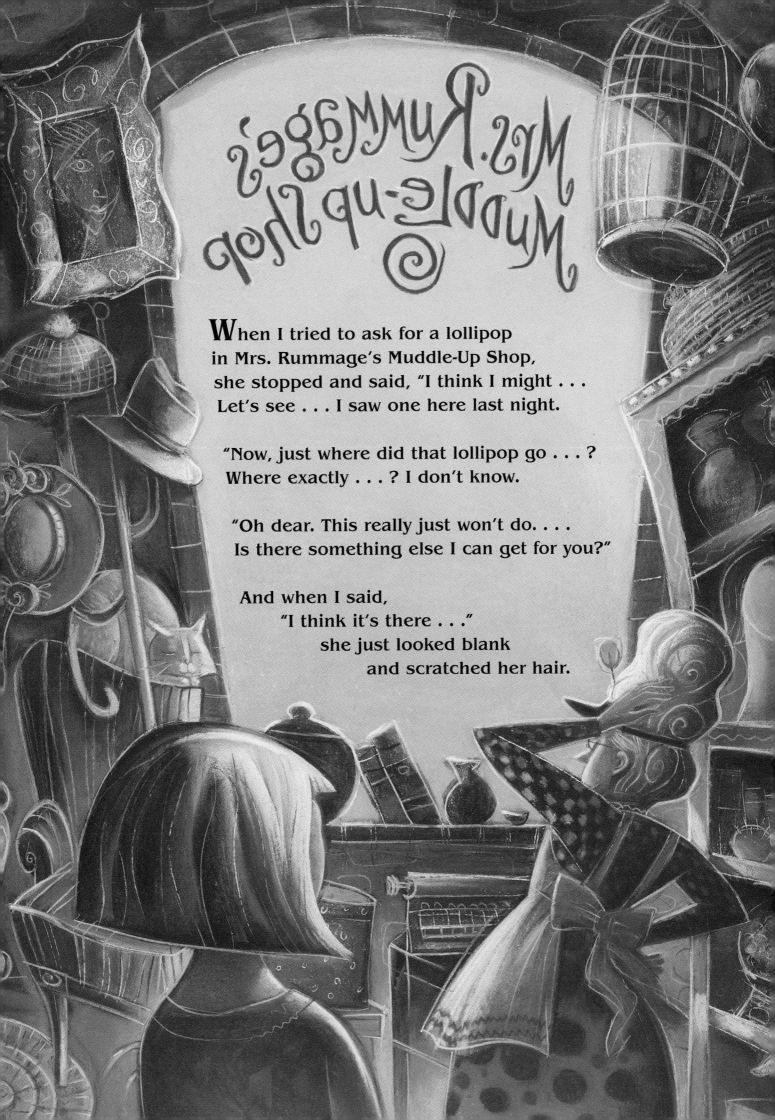

"Now where," she said, "in a Muddle-Up Shop,
would you go looking for a lollipop?"

And she pulled things out and let them go
as she started to rummage high and low:

"Over here with the diving gear?

Under there with the underwear?

Up on top with the soda pop?

Down below where the loo-rolls go?

In that box with the fancy socks?

In this tin with the buttons in?

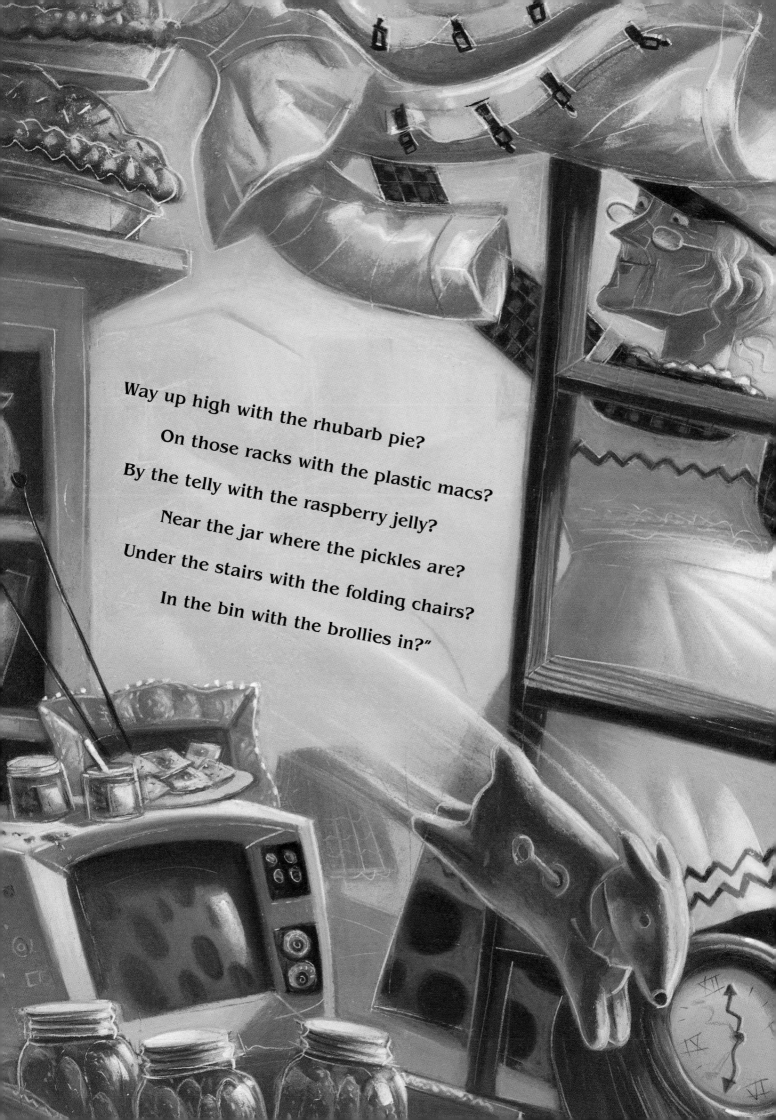

Way up high with the rhubarb pie?
On those racks with the plastic macs?
By the telly with the raspberry jelly?
Near the jar where the pickles are?
Under the stairs with the folding chairs?
In the bin with the brollies in?"

And she reached up high
      and she rummaged low
but she wouldn't hear
      when I tried to show.

"Oh dear," she'd say,
      "I'm sure it's here.
How *can* a lollipop disappear?

"Let's have a *really* good look round.
That's the way
      that a lollipop's found . . ."

It's then that I had to shout,
      "PLEASE STOP!
I JUST WANT TO BUY
      THAT LOLLIPOP!"

"Oh, that!" she said.
    "Why, goodness me!
You can have *that* lollipop
    just for free . . .

"That is . . . ," she said,
    with slight distress,
"if you'll help me clear up
    all this mess . . . !"

The Cottage by the Sea

If you go there by day,
out to the ruined cottage
that sits on the cliff,
all you will find is silence.

Perhaps the wind
will pick at a broken shutter,
or maybe a gull
will cry as it flies overhead.

But if you go there by day,
all you will find is stillness
except for a scurry of ants
or maybe a thrush
cracking a snail on a rock.

But if you go there by night
when the moon is low
    and the mist drifts in from the sea,
you may find lights and music,
    noises of joy and laughter
        left over from lives gone by.

But then if you step through the door
to join with the fun,
    everything vanishes, everything closes.
    You'll find yourself standing alone,
    amazed in the darkness,
with everything silent
    and only the wind at your ear.

Instructions for Growing

Shut your eyes.
Open your mind.
Look inside.
What do you find?

Something funny?
Something sad?
Something beautiful,
mysterious, mad?

Open your ears.
Listen well.
A word or phrase
begins to swell?

Catch its rhythm.
Hold its sound.
Gently, slowly
roll it round.

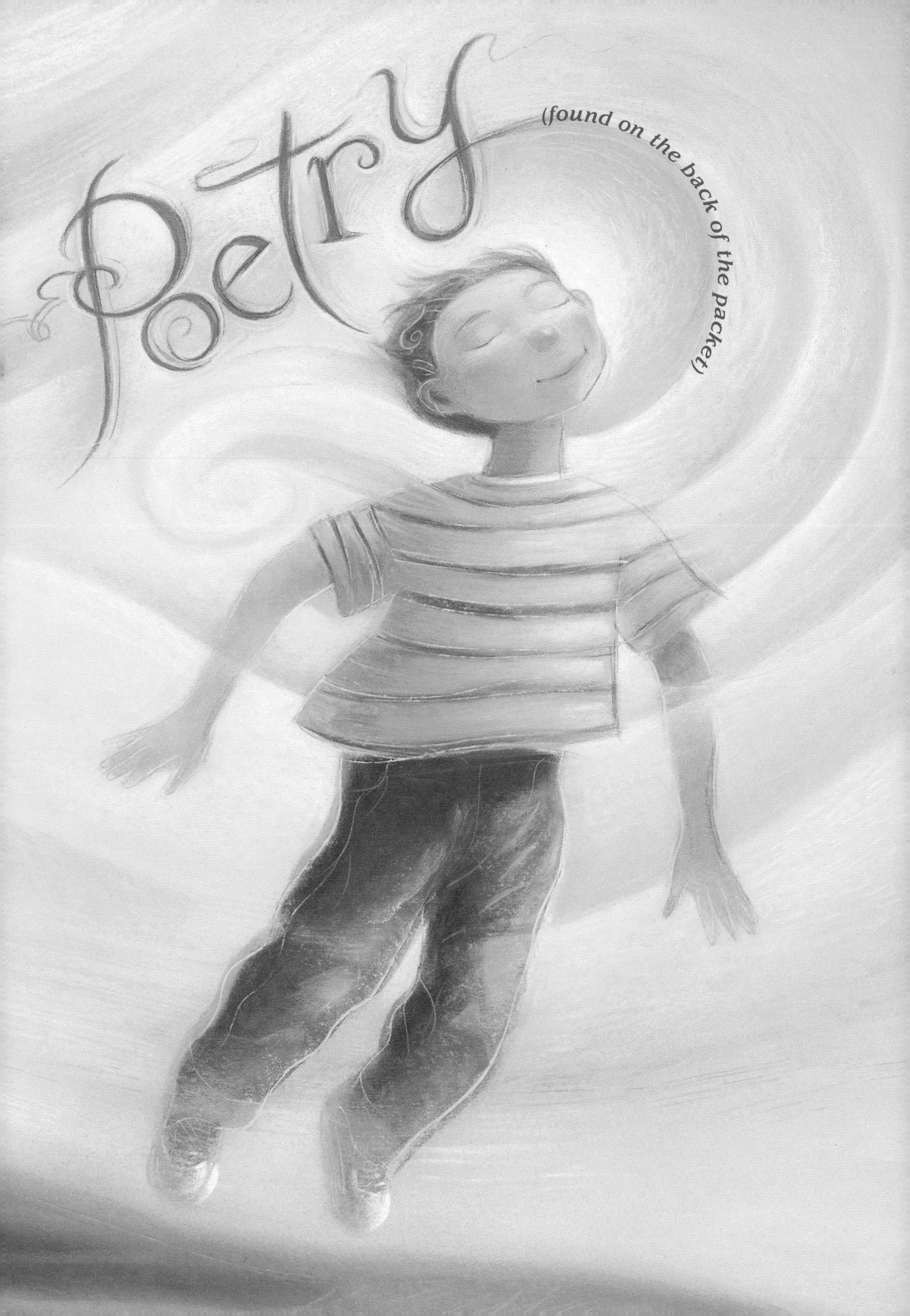
Poetry
(found on the back of the packet)

Does it please you?
      Does it tease you?
      Does it ask
          to grow and spread?

Now those little
      words are sprouting
      poetry
          inside your head.

Notes from the Author

The Histon Boulder

Moses Carter's stone can still be seen in the garden of The Boot public house (pub) in Histon, Cambridgeshire, in England. The distance from The Ballast Hole (a kind of open quarry) to The Boot is by my reckoning a good half mile by way of the road. Moses died in the 1860s and, according to local history, is buried in Histon Churchyard. On my visit there I couldn't find a headstone for him. Perhaps he could not afford one, so he may be glad for this poem to serve instead.

Mrs. Bhattacharya's Chapati Zap Machine

A chapati is a disk-shaped bread from northern India, flat and floppy like a pancake. Poppadoms are thin fried chips the size of dinner plates, made from bean flour and flavored with spices.

The Snake and the Apple

This poem is based on the Bible story in which the serpent tempts Eve with the forbidden fruit (Genesis, Chapter 3, Old Testament).

The Minstrel and the Maid

This is a courtship lyric. The plain print shows the minstrel's voice and the italics show the clever maid's replies.

Green Man Lane

For those readers who have not yet met the Green Man, he is a well-known figure in British folklore. He is often thought to stand for the power of growth in nature. The Green Man's name is preserved on many pub and street signs. His image can be seen in churches all over Europe, carved in wood or stone.

St. Brigid and the Baker

St. Brigid of Ireland has many miracle stories told about her. Often these show her to be kind and generous. Sometimes she manages to increase food and drink to feed unexpected guests. For it was said that, as a young dairymaid, Brigid could draw more milk from a cow than anyone else. She had a special way with the animals.

Song of the Wizard's Imp

It was often thought that witches and wizards had "familiars," strange little animals or creatures who kept them company and helped them with their magic.

Mrs. Rummage's Muddle-Up Shop

A few of the items Mrs. Rummage has in her shop are called by their British names, which may not be familiar to American readers. But Mary GrandPré has drawn them in her pictures. Can you find toilet paper, or "loo-rolls"? A button box, or "button tin"? A raincoat, or "plastic mac"? Some umbrellas, or "brollies"? A television set, or "telly"?